CAPTAIN UNDERPANTS

AND THE BIG, BAD BATTLE OF THE BIONIC BOOGER BOY

PART 1: THE NIGHT OF THE NASTY NOSTRIL NUGGETS

The Sixth Epic Novel b[...]

DAV PILKE[...]

SCHOLASTIC INC.

New York Toronto London Auckland
Mexico City New Delhi Hong Kong Bu[...]

This book is being published simultaneously in hardcover by the Blue Sky Press.

ISBN-13: 978-0-439-37610-5 / ISBN-10: 0-439-37610-6

Be sure to check out Dav Pilkey's Extra-Crunchy Web Site O' Fun at
www.pilkey.com.

28 27 26 25 24 23 22 21   10 11 12 13/0

Printed in the United States of America   40

First Scholastic paperback printing, September 2003

FOR AMY AND JODI

CHAPTERS

George and Harold Prowdly Present

THE AWFUL TRUTH ABOUT CAPTAIN UNDERPANTS

A Treehouse Comix Production

Onse upon a time there was two cool kids named George and Harold.

We Da man!

me too.

They had a mean old Prinsipel named Mr. Krupp.

GRRRR

Hey Bubs!

Blah Blah Blah

One time Mr. Krupp punished George and Harold.

You half To OBey my orders

So they got a 3-D Hypno Ring and Hypnotized him.

No way! you must obey us now

ok.

They made him Think he was a Super Hero.

You are now Captain Underpants

Yes master.

It was suposed to be a Joke.

Tra La Laaaa

Ha Ha Ha

...But it got carried to Far.

Im will Go Fight crime now

window ↓

.....Way to Far!!!

Hey come Back Hear Bub!

Tra La Laaa!

Then one day he got atacked by a dandyLion.

Help.

Dont you hate it when that happens?

So George stole some Super Power Juice from a U.F.O.

Ouchy!

and gave it to him.

Down the hach!

GLug GLug GLug

Sudenly, he got Super Powers.

Hey I can FLy now. I RuLe!

OH Great.

Bummer

Nowadays, Whenever mr. Krupp hears anybody snap there fingers...

Snap

...He turns into you-Know-who!

Tra-La-Laaaa!

UH OH

NoT again

And the only way you can stop him is if you pore water on his head.

H2O

what the?

Then he Turns Back into Mr. Krupp.

Hey whats the Big idea Bubs?

So whatever you do, Dont snap your fingers around mr. krupp ok?

THE END

CHAPTER 1

GEORGE AND HAROLD

This is George Beard and Harold Hutchins.
George is the kid on the left with the tie
and the flat-top. Harold is the one on the
right with the T-shirt and the bad haircut.
Remember that now.

George's and Harold's grades in school were much like whales in the ocean: They rarely rose above "C" level.

Melvin Sneedly, however (he's the kid down there with the bow tie and the glasses), always got straight A's.

Because Melvin was so academically gifted, people just assumed he was a lot smarter than George and Harold.

But that wasn't true.

You see, George and Harold were every bit as smart as the *straight A* students . . . but in a *different* way. In a way that couldn't be measured by quizzes or worksheets.

Maybe George and Harold couldn't spell very well or remember their multiplication tables. Perhaps their grammar weren't no good neither. But when it came to saving the entire planet from the nasty forces of unrelenting evil, there was nobody better than George Beard and Harold Hutchins.

It's a good thing that George and Harold
were smart enough to get themselves out of
trouble, because their silliness was always
getting them *into* trouble. In fact, one time
it got them into a really *SNOTTY* situation.

But before I can tell you that story, I have
to tell you *this* story. . . .

CHAPTER 2
SQUISHIES, PART 1

It was Demonstration Speech Day in Ms. Ribble's fourth-grade English class. Every student had to give an oral report demonstrating how to do something. First up were Tim Bronski and Stevie Loopner, who demonstrated how to give a speech that they hadn't prepared for.

They got a D-.

Next up were Jessica Gordon and Stephanie Wycoff, who demonstrated how to cook frozen lasagna in a pop-up toaster.

After the firemen left, it was George and Harold's turn. Harold carefully tacked some charts and graphs onto the wall while George brought out a large garbage can with a toilet seat taped to the top.

SIDe veiw

SQUISHIES
① kechup ② kechup ③

CROSS Seckshon

seat

← BUMPY Thingy
← kechup
← BOWL

SIDE VEi...

"Ladies and gentlemen," said George.
"Today Harold and I are going to demonstrate how to do a 'Squishy.' First, you need
two packs of ketchup and a toilet seat."

"Next," said Harold as he pointed to their
display chart, "you must fold the ketchup
packs in half and carefully place them under
the toilet seat. Make sure that the packs are
under those front two bumpy thingies on
the bottom of the seat."

"Now, once the ketchup packs are in place," said Harold, "all you have to do is wait for somebody to sit down on the toilet seat. Do we have any volunteers?"

"C'mon," said George, "who wants a Squishy?"

Although nobody in the class wanted to sit on the toilet seat, everybody wanted to see what would happen if somebody actually DID. So George grasped one side of the toilet seat, Harold grasped the other, and together they pushed down.

SPLAT!!! SPLAT!!!

SPLAT

Everyone in the class was thrilled
(except for the two kids sitting directly in
front of the toilet seat, who were somewhat
less-than-thrilled). "Hooray for Squishies!"
the children shouted.

Now, normally George and Harold's
teacher, Ms. Ribble, would have been very
angry about this particular demonstration
speech.

She would have yelled on and on about "imitateable behavior" and how it's not nice to spray ketchup into people's underwear. But Ms. Ribble had changed quite a bit since the last book, and now she was all about FUN!

"C'mon, kids," shouted Ms. Ribble. "Let's all run to the cafeteria and grab some ketchup packs! Squishies for EVERYBODY!!!"

"HOORAY!" cried the children as they bounded from their seats and dashed toward the classroom door.

"NOT SO FAST!" shouted Melvin Sneedly,
who stood blocking the door with his arms
spread defiantly. "You guys are *so* immature!"

CHAPTER 3

THE COMBINE-O-TRON 2000

Melvin Sneedly, the school brainiac, was not about to let anybody leave the classroom until he had given his demonstration speech.

"We still have fifteen minutes left before lunch," said Melvin, "and that's just enough time for me to demonstrate my new invention, the Combine-O-Tron 2000."

"Aww, *maaaan*!" whined Melvin's classmates.

The children all slumped back into their seats while Melvin pushed a plastic rolling cart to the front of the classroom. On top of the cart were a hamster, a small robot (which Melvin had built himself), and a strange-looking contraption shaped like an ice-cream cone.

"Today," said Melvin, "I will demonstrate how to turn an ordinary hamster into your very own bionic cyber-slave."

Melvin placed his pet hamster, Sulu, at one end of the cart, and his tiny homemade robot at the other end. "I shall now combine this ordinary hamster with this tiny robot using the Combine-O-Tron 2000."

Melvin picked up the Combine-O-Tron 2000 and turned it on. A high-pitched tone pierced the classroom air, getting higher and higher in frequency as the machine charged to full power. Melvin typed some last-minute calculations into the keyboard on the side of the Combine-O-Tron 2000 as its laser extractor warmed up.

Suddenly, two streaks of red glowing light flashed onto Sulu and the tiny robot. The Combine-O-Tron 2000 began assimilating information on the two elements it was about to combine. "Don't worry, kids," said Melvin. "This procedure is totally painless. Sulu won't feel a thing." Finally, a computerized voice started the countdown:

"Combining two elements in five seconds. Combining two elements in four seconds. Combining two elements in three seconds. Combining two elements in two seconds. Combining two elements in one second."

BLAZZZZT!

A burst of brilliant white light shot out
of the Combine-O-Tron 2000 and formed a
ball of energy between Sulu and the tiny
robot. The hamster and the robot began to
slide closer and closer together until they
disappeared into the energy ball.

The smell of burned matches and pickle relish filled the air as hot blasts of electric wind knocked books off of shelves and sent papers flying. Suddenly, there was a blinding flash of light, a quick puff of smoke, and it was all over.

Melvin pulled off his goggles. No longer were a hamster and a robot sitting on the cart before him. Now the hamster and robot were one. Combined at a cellular level. The world's first self-contained, warm-blooded, fuzzy bionic cyborg.

"EUREKA!" shouted Melvin. "IT WORKED! I have created a cybernetic life-form."

The children looked on as Melvin waved a metal detector over the hamster and the reading went off the chart. One of the children raised his hand with a question.

"Yes!" said Melvin enthusiastically.

"Can we go to the lunchroom and get our ketchup packs now?"

"Bu—NO!" screamed Melvin. "Will you forget about Squishies for ONE MINUTE?!!? I've just created the world's first cybernetic hamster, and nobody is leaving this room until I've demonstrated his undying obedience!"

CHAPTER 4
BAD SULU

Sulu didn't seem to know that he had just undergone a groundbreaking transformation. He didn't act any different. He just wandered across the top of the plastic rolling cart sniffing everything around him, only stopping occasionally to scratch his ears or rub his whiskers. But poor Sulu was in for a big surprise.

"Sulu," said Melvin, "I am your master, and you will obey my commands. I want you to demonstrate your new powers for the class. Do a super-bionic jump across the room."

Sulu did not respond.

SNIFF
SNIFF

"Sulu!" said Melvin sternly. "Crush that plastic rolling cart in your bare paws!"

Sulu did not respond.

"SULU!" Melvin shouted. "Go outside, pick up a car, and throw it across the parking lot!"

Sulu did not respond.

Finally, Melvin reached into his book bag and took out a red Ping-Pong paddle he had designed especially for this occasion. "Sulu," he said angrily, "do as I say, or you're going to get a good spanking!"

This time, Sulu did
respond. When he saw the Ping-Pong paddle
he became very frightened, and his little
hamster instincts took over. Sulu jumped
into the air, grabbed the Ping-Pong paddle in
his right paw, and then yanked Melvin onto
the plastic rolling cart with his left paw.

The children finally stopped thinking
about ketchup packs and toilets for a
moment and settled in to watch the show.

CHAPTER 5

THE INCREDIBLY GRAPHIC VIOLENCE CHAPTER, PART 1 (IN FLIP-O-RAMA™)

WARNING:

The following chapter contains graphic depictions of a mean little boy getting spanked by a bionic hamster. While this event is presented for humorous effect, the producers of this book acknowledge that hamster attacks are no laughing matter. If you or someone you love has been the victim of a hamster attack, we strongly urge you to get help by seeking out a local support group in your area, or by visiting www.whenhamstersattack.com.

PILKEY® BRAND
O·RAMA

HERE'S HOW IT WORKS!

STEP 1
First, place your *left* hand inside the dotted lines marked "LEFT HAND HERE." Hold the book open *flat*.

STEP 2
Grasp the *right-hand* page with your right thumb and index finger (inside the dotted lines marked "RIGHT THUMB HERE").

STEP 3
Now *quickly* flip the right-hand page back and forth until the picture appears to be *animated*.

(For extra fun, try adding your own sound-effects!)

FLIP-O-RAMA 1

(pages 41 and 43)

Remember, flip *only* page 41.
While you are flipping, be sure you
can see the picture on page 41
and the one on page 43.
If you flip quickly, the two
pictures will start to look like
<u>one</u> *animated* picture.

Don't forget to
add your own sound-effects!

LEFT HAND HERE

SPANKS FOR
THE MEMORIES

RIGHT
THUMB
HERE

SPANKS FOR
THE MEMORIES

CHAPTER 6

THE AFTERMATH

Although Sulu hadn't *really* spanked Melvin very hard, Melvin wailed and blubbered and carried on anyway.

"You're a BAD hamster!" Melvin cried. "I never want to see you again as long as I live!"

Melvin ran out of the classroom sobbing.
The rest of the class, including Ms. Ribble,
followed him out laughing and chanting,
"Squish-ies, Squish-ies, Squish-ies!" But
George and Harold stayed behind to
comfort the forgotten hamster.

"Don't feel bad, Sulu," said George.
"Melvin is a real meanie!"

"Yeah," said Harold. "Do you want to
come home with us? You can live up in our
tree house."

Sulu jumped onto Harold's shoulder and licked his face. Then he jumped over to George's shoulder and licked his face, too.

"I think we've just adopted a bionic hamster," said Harold.

So George tucked their new pal into his shirt pocket, and the three friends went off to lunch.

CHAPTER 7
MR. KRUPP

About that very same time, the school principal, Mr. Krupp, came marching into the office in a particularly foul mood. He stopped beside Miss Anthrope's desk, huffing and puffing.

"Where's my coffee, Edith?" he shouted.

"Get it yourself, tubby!" Miss Anthrope shouted back.

"I don't need your lip today, woman!" Mr. Krupp growled. "I just want my coffee and I want it NOW!"

"Well, get me a cup, too, while you're at it," Miss Anthrope growled back.

"Aaaaugh!" screamed Mr. Krupp in frustration as he grabbed a newspaper and headed for the faculty restroom. Ms. Ribble was standing beside the restroom door smiling and trying very hard not to laugh.

"What are *you* lookin' at?" Mr. Krupp
snarled as he pushed his way past Ms. Ribble
and slammed the restroom door behind
him. Inside the restroom, you could hear
the faint sound of a belt buckle jingling, a
zipper unzipping, some clothes rustling,
and finally . . .

SPLAT!!! SPLAT!!!

"WHAT THE—!" screamed Mr. Krupp from inside the restroom. "I'VE GOT KETCHUP IN MY UNDERWEAR!!!"

In a few moments, the door of the
faculty restroom flew open. "I'm going to
get George and Harold for this!" Mr. Krupp
screamed.

"They didn't do it," laughed Ms. Ribble. "I
did! It's called a *Squishy*. It's the latest fad!"

"Yeah, right. Very funny!" said Mr. Krupp.
"Now, where are those two kids? I just *KNOW*
they're responsible!"

As Mr. Krupp headed for the cafeteria, he noticed that he wasn't the only person to fall victim to the dreaded Squishies. All through the hallway, angry first, second, third, fifth, and sixth graders were complaining about ketchup stains on their pants, socks, legs, and underwear. Mr. Krupp stormed into the cafeteria and headed for the fourth graders' table.

"George and Harold!" shouted Mr. Krupp.
"I've got ketchup in my underwear because
of you two. And so do half of the kids in
this school!"

"We didn't do it," said Harold.

"Yeah," said a few of the other fourth
graders. "George and Harold are innocent."

"Oh no they're NOT," said a voice from the other end of the table. It was Melvin Sneedly. Besides being the school brainiac, Melvin was also famous for being the school tattletale. "George and Harold taught every-body a trick today where you put ketchup packs under a toilet seat and make it spray on people's legs," Melvin reported proudly.

"Thank you, Melvin," said Mr. Krupp. He turned to George and Harold and pointed at the cafeteria door. "Mr. Beard and Mr. Hutchins—OUT!"

CHAPTER 8

THE COMIC IS MIGHTIER THAN THE SPITBALL

George and Harold were sent straight to the detention room.

"Man," said Harold, "Melvin is such a tattletale. Somebody ought to teach him a lesson."

"And we're just the guys to do it," said George.

So George and Harold created an all-new comic book featuring everybody's favorite tattletalin' meanie, Melvin Sneedly. When they were done, the two boys sneaked out of the detention room to run off copies of their latest work and sell them in the hallway.

The new comic book was a great
success. Everybody loved it. Well, everybody but Melvin Sneedly, I should say. As
Melvin walked to his last class of the day,
he noticed small groups of students in
the hallway reading comics together and
giggling. Normally, this was enough to
make Melvin run straight to the principal's
office and tell on everyone for unsupervised
reading (which was strictly forbidden). But
today, Melvin noticed something strange.
The comic-reading students were pointing
and laughing—at HIM.

"What?" said Melvin. "What's wrong? What are you guys laughing at?" Melvin looked around the hallway desperately. Everybody was laughing . . . everybody was pointing . . . and it was driving Melvin crazy! He marched over to a group of second graders, grabbed the comic book out of their hands, and looked at the cover. Melvin was FURIOUS!

"YOU GUYS ARE *SO* IMMATURE!!!"
shrieked Melvin. He quickly darted off to
read the comic in peace, but everywhere he
ran, he came across more pointing and more
laughing. Finally, Melvin thought of the one
place he could read the comic in private. He
went into the boys' bathroom, locked himself
in one of the stalls, and sat down to read.

SPLAT!!! SPLAT!!!

As Melvin sat reading, his legs dripping with ketchup, he became angrier and angrier. "I'm gonna get George and Harold!" Melvin vowed.

CHAPTER 9

CAPTAIN UNDERPANTS AND THE TERRIFYING TALE OF THE TATTLE-TRON 2000

Duh.

BY GEORGE BEARD AND HAROLD HUTCHINS

CAPTAIN UNDERPANTS
AND THE TERIFYING TALE
OF THE TATTLE-TRON 2000

By George Beard and Harold Hutchins

Onse Upon a time There was a dumb Kid named Melvin Who was a big Tattle-tale.

I'm Telling

KEEP OFF THE GRASS

Everywhare He went he caUsed GreiF and Mizery.

Im Telling

NO SKATE BORDING

Until one Day...

BANK

I'm Telling

$

CRASH

Hey cops, That guy JUST Robed the Bank.

Gee Thanks Kid.

$

You're are under a rest.

Hey KID you solved the Crime of The senchery!

And So...

Daily News

DUMB KiD is a Hero

Everybody Loves MELvIN!!!

Melvin had became so populer that he desided to run for Mayer.

Melvin 4 Mayer

VOTE 4 Melvin

Im TELLING

CON-FETY

VOTE 4 A HERO

MELvin 4 MAyer

my Hero

He won in a Landslide Victery

Daily NEWS

DUMB KiD Becomes MAyER

Congrajew-Lashons!!! Your the Youngest Mayer ever!

Yes and Im going To make BiG Changes!

Mayer

Soon Mayor Melvin made a bunch of Dumb new Laws.

And people were getting arested Left and Right

And they all got sent to Jail

Sudenly...

Mayer Melvin. ALL The Jails are full!

Hmm

Mayer

I will Build a big Robo-Jail and catch those Lawbrakers myself!

So he built the Tattle-Tron 2000

CLANG CLANG

Soon Mayer Melvin was off catching Lawbreakers.

No old Ladies

that'LL teach you!

Then Melvin Headed For the school.

Help! The Tattle-Tron 2000 Just Ran across the soccer Feild and squished the Gym Teacher!

OH NO! We just PLanted that grass!

Prinsiple

This Looks Like a JoB For...

Prinsiple

CRASH

CAPTAIN UNderPANtS!

Your going to Jail for Busting The Roof!

But Captain Underpants was Faster than a speeding waistband...

More Powerful Than Boxer shorts...

And able To Leap Tall Buildings Without getting a wedgie.

captain Underpants wanted to fight the Robot but he dident want to hurt the people inside.

Then he got a idea.

mrs. Plops PRUNE JUICE FACKTORY

mrs. Plops PRUNE JUICE FACKTERY

Prune Juice

CRASH

"It makes you go poop"

Hey!

Prune Juice

What the ???

UH-OH

Soon there was no-body left inside the Tattle-Tron 2000 exsept for Melvin.

And so....

Then everybody got sent Fr
TRA-La-Laaaaa!!!
Man Jail
Lady Jail
Kid Jail
Baby Jail
Dog Jail
Cat Jail
Frog Jail
RiBiT
MeoW
were free and stuff!
Yaay
Yipee
Goo-Goo
RUFF
THE END!!
TreeHouse
Comix Inc.

CHAPTER 10
MAD MR. MELVIN

Melvin was furious. He ripped the comic book in half and tossed it over his shoulder. Then he washed his hands in the toilet and stormed out of the restroom.

"I'm gonna get George and Harold for that," said Melvin. "I'm gonna teach them a lesson they'll NEVER forget!"

After school, Melvin grabbed his Combine-O-Tron 2000 and headed home.

Melvin's mother and father were both busy working on a top-secret government experiment when Melvin walked in the front door.

"Hello, son," said Melvin's father. "How was your day at school?"

"Terrible!" said Melvin. "Nobody in school has sufficient respect for my beautiful mind. Those dull-witted, lame-brained, gum-chewing idiots are more impressed with comic books than they are with the wonders of science. But I shall teach them. I shall teach them all! Ha-ha-ha-ha-haaaa!"

"That's nice, honey," said Melvin's mom.

Melvin marched up to his room to begin
building a brand-new super-powered robot.
But when he opened his bedroom door, he
saw the family's pet cat, Danderella, sleeping
quietly on his bed.

"Hey!" Melvin screamed. "What are you
doing in my room, you stupid cat? You know
I'm allergic to you! Now get out and—a—a—
A-Chooo!—STAY OUT!"

After a few hours, Melvin had built his newest and most powerful robot ever, which had three sets of interchangeable laser eyeballs, Macro-Hydraulic Jump-A-Tronic legs, Super-Somgobulating Automo-Arms, and an extendable Octo-Claw rib cage, and was powered by three separate Twin Turbo-9000 SP5 Kung-Fu Titanium/Lithium Alloy Processors, which were all built into a virtually indestructible Flexo-Growmonic endoskeleton that had the power to punch through cinder blocks, crush steel in its vise-like grasp, and plow mercilessly through poorly written run-on sentences.

It could also slice bagels.

"That ought to do the trick," said Melvin, wiping his nose on a tissue. "Now, all I have to do is—a—a—A-Chooo!—combine my body with this bionic robot, and I shall be the most powerful boy who—a—a—A-Chooo!— ever lived!"

CHAPTER 11
MELVIN'S FANTASY

As Melvin set up the Combine-O-Tron 2000 and made the proper adjustments, he imagined what his life would be like as the world's first bionic boy. He imagined himself walking into school the next day, his arms swinging confidently as he crashed through the classroom wall.

The girls would swoon as Melvin talked
for hours about the amazing world of
science. Ms. Ribble would probably let Melvin
sit at her desk from now on, because Melvin's
new buns of steel would be too massive to
fit into an ordinary children's chair.

Maybe Mr. Krupp would invite the governor to visit the school, so he could show off his smartest and most powerful student. If so, the governor would probably declare a new holiday, "National Melvin Sneedly Day": a day when kids all over the world would get extra homework and pop quizzes to honor the glorious name of Melvin.

But the best part of all would be George
and Harold's reaction. They would be so
terrified by Melvin's incredible size and
strength, they'd drop to their knees and beg
for mercy. And Melvin would spare them only
if they agreed to be his slaves for all eternity.
They'd have to carry his books, sharpen his
pencils, and be his personal footstools
during each class.

"Life is gonna—a—a—A-Chooo!—
RULE!" said Melvin.

CHAPTER 12

THE NIGHT OF THE NASTY NOSTRIL NUGGETS

Melvin turned on the Combine-O-Tron 2000. A high-pitched tone pierced the air, getting higher and higher in frequency as the machine charged to full power. "Oops," said Melvin as he quickly turned the *Dramatic Effects* setting to "off" so he wouldn't disturb his parents. Silently, the machine continued to charge as Melvin entered calculations to account for his clothes and glasses. When the laser extractor had finally warmed up, Melvin stepped in front of the Combine-O-Tron 2000, standing perfectly still beside his new robot.

Suddenly, two streaks of red glowing light flashed onto Melvin and the robot as the Combine-O-Tron 2000 began assimilating information on the two elements it was about to combine. Finally, a computerized voice started the countdown:

"Combining two elements in five seconds."

Melvin stood perfectly still.

"Combining two elements in four seconds."

Melvin's nose began to twitch.

"Combining two elements in three seconds."

Suddenly, Melvin felt an uncontrollable urge. He cupped his hands over his mouth and nose as his eyes squeezed closed involuntarily. "A—a—a . . ."

"Combining two elements in two seconds."

"—A-Chooo!" Melvin looked down into his hands, which were now glistening with mucus and crusty chunks of semi-dried booglets. Instantly, the Combine-O-Tron 2000 began to recalculate the elements in its laser sights.

"Combining three elements in one second."

"THREE elements?" Melvin screamed in horror. "W-W-What's the THIRD ELEMENT???"

Quickly, Melvin's eyes darted around the room, searching for any new element that might have accidentally made its way into the sights of the laser extractor.

"WHAT'S THE THIRD ELEMENT???" he screamed again. Then he looked down into his crusty, dripping, phlegm-filled hands.

"Uh-oh," said Melvin as a blinding burst of white light enveloped him.

BLAZZZZT!

CHAPTER 13

THE NEXT DAY

The next day, Melvin didn't show up for school on time. Nobody really seemed to notice, though, because all the children were excited about show-and-tell. Almost everyone had brought in really lame stuff like books or awards, but George and Harold had something that was totally *cool*.

"Everybody remembers Sulu from yesterday, right?" said George. "Well, we took him home to live with us in our tree house."

"And we taught him the greatest trick!" said Harold.

The two boys carried Sulu over to the classroom window and opened it up. Harold pulled a large watermelon out of his book bag and showed it to Sulu.

"O.K., Sulu," said George, "show everybody your new trick!"

In one swift motion, Sulu placed his mouth onto the watermelon and shoved the entire thing into his left cheek. The fourth graders were stunned.

"No, no," said Harold, "that's not the trick. The trick is what happens next!"

Sulu looked out the window and eyed
a dead tree at the far end of the empty
playground. Sulu began to chew up the
watermelon, then puckered his tiny
hamster lips and spit.

Ratatatatatatatatatatatatatatat!

The watermelon seeds fired out of Sulu's mouth, hitting their target with expert precision. In no time at all, the dead tree at the end of the playground was reduced to a pile of twigs and sawdust. The class cheered as George and Harold petted their amazing little bionic buddy.

George and Harold didn't think that anybody could beat their show-and-tell display, but they were wrong. Because at that very moment, Melvin Sneedly was dripping down the hallway toward the classroom door. Melvin hadn't brought anything for show-and-tell. Melvin WAS the show-and-tell.

CHAPTER 14

THE UNNECESSARILY DISGUSTING CHAPTER

NOTICE:

The following chapter is
extremely gross.

To avoid nausea, projectile
vomiting, or other gastrointestinal
unpleasantries, please refrain
from eating for at least
one hour before
reading this chapter.

(You won't want to eat after
reading it, let me assure you.)

All of the fourth graders were cheering and petting Sulu as the classroom door slowly opened. A greenish, glistening behemoth entered the room, filling the air with the sounds of grinding metal gears and wet, gooey, bursting bubbles. Some of the girls screamed. Some of the boys did, too.

"You guys are *so* immature!" said the horrible beast.

At once, the children recognized the terrifying creature that stood before them.

"MELVIN?!!?" they cried.

"Yes, it's me," gurgled the wet, jiggling monster angrily. His eyes and nose were dripping with warm, greenish, custard-like mucus. His robotic arms were caked with massive globs of crispy, shimmering snot. And as he turned to close the classroom door behind him, part of his hand came off on the doorknob. It oozed slowly down the door, leaving behind a chunky trail of moist excretion.

Melvin squished and sloshed as he jiggled over to his chair. Each gooey footstep coated the floor with a foamy trail of slime, and everything he touched became wet and encrusted with warm, bubbling, syrupy phlegm.

When Melvin sat down, generous helpings of yellowish, pudding-like goo slowly dribbled down the chair, collecting into creamy,

gelatinous puddles beneath him. The puddles themselves were slightly transparent and speckled with thick, shimmering nose hairs and dark red chunks of coagulated blood, which—

"ALRIGHT ALREADY!" yelled George to the narrator. "Enough with the descriptions—you're making us all sick!"

"Thank you, George," said Ms. Ribble. "Now, Melvin, why don't you tell us all what happened to you?"

"Well," said Melvin, "I tried to combine myself with a bionic robot last night, but I accidentally sneezed at the last second."

"So you got combined with a robot—and *boogers*?" asked George.

"Yeah," said Melvin. "But don't worry, I'm building a Separatron 1000, which will reverse the effects and turn me back into a boy again. It'll just take six months to finish."

"Six *MONTHS*?" said Harold.

"Hey, cellular separation is a highly complex procedure," said Melvin. "It's not like building a robot. It takes time!"

"You should try taking the batteries out of that Combine-O-Thingy and putting them in backward," suggested George. "That might reverse the effect."

Melvin rolled his thick, bubbling, crust-covered infrared eyeballs. "That's the dumbest thing I've ever heard!" he gurgled.

CHAPTER 15

THE NEW MELVIN

You might think that turning into a Bionic Booger Boy was the worst thing that could ever happen to a kid, but it wasn't all bad. Believe it or not, there was actually a positive side to being a lumbering loogie lad. For instance, Melvin now won every football game he played . . . because no one wanted to tackle him.

And when he served a volleyball, nobody
on the other team would dare to hit the
ball back.

Besides being the school's new sports star, there were other perks, too. Melvin never had to wait in line at the drinking fountain anymore. Now he had his own *personal* drinking fountain, because . . . well, would *you* use a drinking fountain after a Bionic Booger Boy had globbered all over it?

I didn't think so.

All of the special attention that Melvin was receiving made some of the other kids a little jealous. But not George and Harold. Considering the many evil villains that George and Harold had been battling all year, the two boys were just grateful that Melvin hadn't turned himself into a gigantic, terrifying beast with plans to destroy the earth.

"It could be a LOT worse," said Harold.
"At least Melvin's not a terrifying evil villain."

"Yeah, you're right," said George. "I can't
think of *anything* that could turn Melvin
into a terrifying evil villain. . . . "

CHAPTER 16

THE COLD AND FLU SEASON

Soon it was autumn, and the new season brought with it many changes: crisp, chilly air; early morning frost; and bright, colorful leaves. But with the beauty of autumn came another change that wasn't quite so welcome: *the cold and flu season*.

All through Jerome Horwitz Elementary School, people were getting sick. The hallways were filled with runny noses, sneezing mouths, and aching bodies.

SNIFF   A-CHOOO   SNIFF SNIFF

SNIFF

And unfortunately, one of those noses, mouths, and bodies belonged to Melvin Sneedly.

Every time Melvin sneezed, thousands of tiny driblets shot out of his mouth,

spattering the chalkboard with a thin
layer of foamy, glistening, yellowish-green,
tapioca-like mucus.

"Don't forget to cover your mouth,
Melvin, dear," said Ms. Ribble.

"Oh, sorry," said Melvin. "Sorry." He put his hand over his mouth and sneezed again. This time, the explosion of air from his stifled sneeze blew off large, wet globs of his body, which sprayed over the entire classroom.

It was as if somebody set off a giant fire-cracker inside a bucket of green paint. The warm, smelly goo smacked into people's hair, splattered onto their clothes, and seemed to drench every square inch of the room.

"On second thought, Melvin," said Ms. Ribble, "*don't* cover your mouth next time. Now, who wants a cookie?"

CHAPTER 17

THE FIELD TRIP

The next day, for some strange reason, Ms. Ribble was out sick with a cold. Mr. Krupp was filling in as the substitute teacher and, as usual, he was very angry.

"What the *heck* is going on in this room?" he yelled. "What's with all the raincoats and umbrellas?"

Then Melvin sneezed.

A few moments later, Mr. Krupp returned to the classroom with fresh clothes, a rain-coat, and an umbrella. "Alright everybody," he shouted. "Today is Field Trip Day. Miss Anthrope and I are taking you all to Snoddy Bros. Tissue Factory to see how blow-rags are made."

The word "tissue" made Melvin jump. "NO!" he cried in a panic. "ME NO LIKE TISSUES!"

An eerie silence fell over the classroom. Everybody looked at Melvin in shock.

"Did Melvin just say *me no like tissues*?" asked Harold.

"Yeah," said George. "I've never heard him misuse an objective pronoun before. Who does he think he is, *Frankenstein*?"

CHAPTER 18

THINGS GET BAD

In a few hours, the fourth graders were all
packed into a hot, stinky factory listening to
a boring speech about how trees are turned
into tissues . . . or something like that.
Nobody was paying attention, really, except
for Melvin Sneedly, who was terrified. His
whole body shook and shimmered as the tour
took them down the narrow walkways of the
noisy industrial plant.

DANGER

BORING
TOUR
AHEAD

Finally, the tour ended at the gift shop, where the plant manager, Mr. Snoddy, had a surprise for everybody.

"Behind this red curtain with black dots on it," said Mr. Snoddy, "is a free gift for each of you." Mr. Snoddy pulled back the curtain to reveal a pile of sample tissue packs. "Help yourselves," said Mr. Snoddy. "There's enough for everybody!"

"NOOOOO!" screamed Melvin. "ME NO LIKE TISSUES!"

"Oh, don't be silly," said Mr. Snoddy. "Everybody *loves* tissues. And our tissues are extra absorbent. They really help to wipe out phlegm and mucus!"

"NOOOOO!" screamed Melvin again. "TISSUES IS *BAD MAGIC*!"

"Nonsense," laughed Mr. Snoddy. He tossed a couple of sample tissue packs at Melvin. "Here you go, young man," he said. "Enjoy!"

The tissue packs flipped through the air and stuck onto Melvin's back. Melvin screamed. His eyes began to glow green as he beat his chest in anger. Suddenly, Melvin's shoulders started to bubble. His chest expanded. The Flexo-Growmonic steel in Melvin's endoskeleton flexed and grew. His neck and head widened, and his body swelled to a height of thirteen feet.

Melvin grabbed the tissue packs in his
massive, dripping fingers and flung them
to the ground. "DON'T MAKE ME ANGRY!"
Melvin warned. "YOU NO LIKE ME WHEN
I ANGRY!"

"Oops," said Mr. Snoddy. "You dropped
your tissue packs, young fellow. Here's some
more for you!" Mr. Snoddy grabbed two giant
handfuls of sample tissue packs and tossed
them at Melvin.

CHAPTER 19

THINGS GET BADDER

Frantically, Melvin swatted at the nine new tissue packs stuck to his upper torso as if they were a swarm of stinging bumblebees. He stomped his giant spiked feet and thrashed about violently as his hulking body doubled, then *tripled* in size. Melvin kicked and punched the walls of the gift shop as he let out a terrifying, bloodcurdling cry.

"There's no need to cry, little man,"
said Mr. Snoddy. "Here—have some more
tissues to dry those tears!" He tossed several
more sample tissue packs at Melvin. (As
you might have noticed by now, Mr. Snoddy
wasn't exactly the brightest bulb on the
Hanukkah tree.)

What happened next could only be
described as chaos. Once again, Melvin's
massive body tripled in size. By now, Melvin
was roaring and kicking and knocking over
giant machines. Children screamed and ran.

Mr. Snoddy thought it might help matters if he could just give Melvin some more tissues. But before he could, a drop of mucus the size of a bathtub dripped from Melvin's massive nose and splashed down on Mr. Snoddy, gluing him to the floor.

George and Harold hid behind the red
curtain with black dots on it as Melvin
crashed through the roof of the factory. Ear-
piercing roars bellowed out of his gigantic,
oozing mouth as he kicked down the walls
of the factory and tossed heavy machinery
into the parking lot. Mr. Krupp and Miss
Anthrope tried their best to get the situation
under control, but they weren't having
much luck.

"Hey, bub," shouted Mr. Krupp, "I've had just about enough of your shenanigans!"

"You're gonna be spending the afternoon in detention if you don't settle down, young man!" shouted Miss Anthrope.

Suddenly, Melvin reached down and grabbed Miss Anthrope in his massive metal fist.

"HELP ME!" she screamed. "SOMEBODY SAVE ME!"

"Uh . . . ummm . . ." said Mr. Krupp nervously, "I'll—I'll go get some help!"

Mr. Krupp ran and hid with George and Harold behind the red curtain with black dots on it.

"Hey, I thought you were going to go get some help!" said Harold.

"Well, not *today*," said Mr. Krupp.

"You know," said George, "there's only one person who can help Miss Anthrope now."

"Who's that?" asked Mr. Krupp.

CHAPTER 20

CAPTAIN UNDERPANTS, THAT'S WHO

As much as George and Harold hated to do
it, they decided that it was time to send in
Captain Underpants to save the day.
George snapped his fingers. Suddenly, the
terror and panic that Mr. Krupp had been
experiencing completely vanished.

A wild, silly grin spread across his face
as he leaped to his feet and ripped off his
outer clothing and toupee. Mr. Krupp's
transformation into Captain Underpants
was almost complete. The only thing he
was missing was a cape.

"Gee," he said, "I sure wish I could find
a red curtain with black dots on it."

"Hey," said George as he pointed to
the red curtain with black dots on it,
"here's a red curtain with black dots on it."

"What a remarkably unexpected coinci-
dence," said Captain Underpants as he
grabbed the latest in a series of convoluted
plot devices and tied it around his neck.

By this time, Melvin had stomped his way
out of the factory and into the downtown
area, leaving behind a twisted path of mucus-
coated destruction. Captain Underpants flew
into the air, following the trail of terror until
he was face-to-face with the snot-spewing
cyborg.

"I order you to stop," said Captain
Underpants, "in the name of all that is Pre-
Shrunk and Cottony!" Melvin did not listen.

Captain Underpants had no choice but to fight the boogery behemoth, but first he needed to save Miss Anthrope. Quickly, our hero flew to Edith's side, grabbed her hands, and pulled firmly. The slimy phlegm that covered Melvin's gigantic fist was strong and gluey, but it was no match for Wedgie Power.

Captain Underpants pulled and pulled
until Miss Anthrope became completely
dislodged with a noisy, wet, disgusting
sound. (Note: Please feel free to make the
noisy, wet, disgusting sound of your choice
to emphasize the intense drama of this
gripping paragraph.)

"I'm free!" cried Miss Anthrope. "Let's
get the heck out of here!"

Suddenly, the Bionic Booger Boy reached down and grabbed Captain Underpants by the cape. The monster held on tightly with his gigantic, gooey robotic fingers.

"ACK!" cried Captain Underpants. "He's got my cape! He's got my cape!"

"Well just untie it!" screamed Miss Anthrope. "Let's GO! Let's GO!"

"But I—I can't fight crime without my cape!" cried Captain Underpants.

"FORGET YOUR STUPID CAPE!" Edith screamed. "Just save me, you idiot!"

CHAPTER 21

YOU CAN'T HAVE YOUR CAPE AND EDITH, TOO

As anybody will tell you, no superhero is complete without a cape. I mean, without a cape, a superhero is just a guy wearing fancy underwear (or in this case, *not*-so-fancy underwear). But Captain Underpants knew what had to be done. He reached up with his free hand and courageously untied his cape, valiantly sacrificing his aesthetic integrity to save the life of a mere mortal being.

Captain Underpants and Miss Anthrope
were now free, but they weren't safe yet.
The Bionic Booger Boy swung at our hero
with all his might. Captain Underpants
weaved around Melvin's frantic, flying,
phlegm-flingin' fists as he tried to find a
safe place to land.

Suddenly, Captain Underpants's 100% cotton-powered vision spotted George and Harold miles away. With lightning speed, he flew down to meet the boys.

"George and Harold," said Captain Underpants, "you've got to keep this woman safe while I destroy that robotic slimeball!"

"O.K.," said Harold, "but hurry up—here he comes!"

"Wait," cried Miss Anthrope. "I—I didn't get a chance to say thank you." She turned and kissed Captain Underpants all over his face with wet, drooly smooches.

"Thank you! Thank you! Thank you!" she said between each sloppy kiss.

"Yuck!" said Harold.

"I sure hope she doesn't thank *us*," said George.

When Miss Anthrope had finished slobbering all over Captain Underpants's face, she gave him a great big hug for good luck. "Now go get him, tiger," she said coyly.

But Captain Underpants didn't move. He just stood there staring blankly into space.

Off in the distance, George and Harold could hear the Bionic Booger Boy approaching. Each thundering footstep brought the horrible beast closer and closer, until at last he stood towering above them, panting heavily, and dripping profanely.

Miss Anthrope screamed and ran away.

"Hurry, Captain Underpants!" cried
Harold. "DO SOMETHING!"

"Yeah," cried George. "KICK HIS HINEY!
KICK HIS HINEY!"

But Captain Underpants didn't move. He
didn't fight. He didn't fly. He didn't kick
anybody's hiney. In fact, the only thing he
did do was get very, very angry.

"What the heck is going on here, bubs?"
he screamed. "And why am I standing here
in my underwear?"

George and Harold didn't like the sound
of that.

CHAPTER 22

WELCOME BACK, KRUPPER

If you read the comic on page 7 of this novel, then you know what happens whenever Captain Underpants gets water on his head. Unfortunately, Miss Anthrope's wet, slobbery kisses had produced the same effect.

Captain Underpants had been turned back into Mr. Krupp . . . and now he was about to be turned into *lunch*!

Quickly, George and Harold began
frantically snapping their fingers.

SNAP! SNAP! SNAP! SNAP! SNAP!

Again and again, they snapped. But Mr.
Krupp's face was still slimy and wet with
gooey kiss juice, and the snaps were
having no effect at all.

The mighty mucus monster shoved Mr. Krupp into his gummy mouth and swallowed him whole . . .

. . . and then he came after George and
Harold.

"HELP!" screamed George.

"WE'RE DOOMED!" screamed Harold.

CHAPTER 23

SULU SAVES THE DAY

Halfway across the city, a plucky little hamster with bionic ears heard the terrified cries of his two best pals. Quickly, Sulu jumped out of his exercise wheel and crashed through the side of his plastic cage.

Then, with a mighty leap, he bounded from the window of George and Harold's tree house.

At that very moment, Melvin was dangling George and Harold high above his mouth.

"HAW, HAW, HAW!" laughed the Bionic Booger Boy. "ME GOTS YOU AT LAST!"

"Well, good-bye, Harold," said George.

"See you later, pal," said Harold. "It was fun while it lasted."

Finally, Melvin let go of George and Harold. The two boys screamed as they fell face first into the gooey, gaping mouth of the—

SWOOOOOOOOOOOOSH!

The next thing George and Harold knew, they were flying sideways at an incredible speed. Everything around them was a blur of motion, except for the sight of their little buddy Sulu, who had literally grabbed them from the murky mouth of death at the very last second.

"Atta boy!" cried George.

"Hooray for Sulu!" cried Harold.

Sulu set George and Harold down on the roof of a distant building, then returned to the scene of the crime. He grabbed a few oversize novelty items from the tops of some warehouses and turned to face his mortal enemy.

THE CANE WAREHOUSE

BOXING GLOVE CITY

THE DENTURE EMPORIUM

CHAPTER 24

THE INCREDIBLY GRAPHIC VIOLENCE CHAPTER, PART 2 (IN FLIP-O-RAMA™)

WARNING:

The following stunts were
performed on closed streets
by a highly trained
professional hamster.
To avoid injury,
please do not grab
oversize novelty items
from the tops of
warehouses and beat up
giant monsters
with them.

FLIP-O-RAMA 2

(pages 147 and 149)

Remember, flip *only* page 147.
While you are flipping, be sure you
can see the picture on page 147
and the one on page 149.
If you flip quickly, the two
pictures will start to look like
<u>one</u> *animated* picture.

Don't forget to
add your own sound-effects!

LEFT HAND HERE

CANE TOPS KEEP FALLIN' ON MY HEAD

147

RIGHT THUMB HERE

CANE TOPS KEEP
FALLIN' ON MY HEAD

FLIP-O-RAMA 3

(pages 151 and 153)

Remember, flip *only* page 151.
While you are flipping, be sure you
can see the picture on page 151
and the one on page 153.
If you flip quickly, the two
pictures will start to look like
<u>one</u> *animated* picture.

Don't forget to
add your own sound-effects!

LEFT HAND HERE

YUMMY, YUMMY, YUMMY (I GOT GLOVE IN MY TUMMY)

RIGHT
THUMB
HERE

YUMMY, YUMMY, YUMMY (I GOT GLOVE IN MY TUMMY)

FLIP-O-RAMA 4

(pages 155 and 157)

Remember, flip *only* page 155.
While you are flipping, be sure you
can see the picture on page 155
and the one on page 157.
If you flip quickly, the two
pictures will start to look like
<u>one</u> *animated* picture.

Don't forget to
add your own sound-effects!

LEFT HAND HERE

A HARD DAY'S BITE

A HARD DAY'S BITE

CHAPTER 25

HOW TO REVERSE THE EFFECTS OF A COMBINE-O-TRON 2000 IN ONE EASY STEP

The Bionic Booger Boy was defeated. He flopped, unconscious, into a giant boogery blob that spread across several city blocks (and nearly four whole pages) as reporters surrounded his massive, oozing body.

Soon, Melvin's mother and father showed up with the Combine-O-Tron 2000. "We saw what was happening on the news," they said. "And we want the world to know that we're going to create a new machine that will reverse the process that turned our son into this monster. If we work together, it should only take a few months to build!"

"Why don't you guys just take the batteries out of that *Combine-O-Thingy* and switch 'em around?" said George. "Wouldn't that reverse the machine's effects?"

"Well," laughed Melvin's father, "obviously you don't know anything about science, little boy. You can't expect to reverse the effects of a highly complex cellular-molecularizing Combine-O-Tron just by switching the batteries around. That type of thing only happens in obnoxious children's books."

"Ahem," said George self-consciously. "Well . . . why don't you just give it a try anyway?"

"Alright," said Mr. Sneedly, rolling his eyes and smirking. He quickly switched the batteries around and powered up the machine. "But I'm only doing this to prove a point to you kids: It's not gonna work. No way. Not in a million years. And anybody who thinks it might is a complete idiot. It goes against all the popular laws of logic and science."

He aimed the newly reconfigured Combine-O-Tron 2000 at his son and fired.

CHAPTER 26

BLAZZZZT!

Suddenly, there was a terrific explosion.
The Bionic Booger Boy burst into three huge
chunks of glistening snot and twisted metal,
which smacked onto three nearby buildings
and stuck like glue. In the center of the
explosion, surrounded by smoke, stood Mr.
Krupp and Melvin.

"Well, what do you know?" said Mr.
Sneedly. "My idea worked."

George and Harold rolled their eyes.

"Now, step aside, kiddies," said Mrs. Sneedly as the two scientists marched off to tell the reporters all about their brilliant and inspirational scientific breakthrough.

But as the smoke around Mr. Krupp and
Melvin began to clear, it became obvious
that they were not quite back to normal.
Apparently, the newly reconfigured Combine-
O-Tron 2000 had accidentally morphed Mr.
Krupp and Melvin together.

"Don't worry," Mr. Sneedly told the reporters. "All I need to do is zap them one more time. That should set everything straight!" He fired up the Combine-O-Tron 2000 again and prepared to blast away.

"I sure hope this separates their bodies," said George.

"Me, too," said Harold.

BLAZZZZT!

CHAPTER 27

TO MAKE A LONG STORY SHORT

It did.

CHAPTER 28
A HAPPY ENDING

"You know something?" said George. "This is the first time one of our books actually had a happy ending."

"You're right," said Harold. "Usually they end with you screaming 'Oh, NO!' and me screaming 'Here we go again!' But we got lucky this time, I guess."

"What do you mean, *lucky*?" said Mr. Krupp. "It was *MY* invention that saved the world. You guys are *so* immature!"

"Huh?" said George.

"I want to see both of you bubs in my office PRONTO!" yelled Melvin. "I'm gonna punish you boys so bad, your *kids* will be born with detentions!"

"Whaaaa?" said Harold.

Suddenly, a giant extendable Octo-Claw
reached out from one of the three huge
chunks of boogers. It grabbed the Combine-
O-Tron 2000 out of Mr. Sneedly's hands and
smashed it to smithereens on the ground.
Mr. and Mrs. Sneedly ran away screaming
as the three humongous robotic booger
chunks came to life.

Slowly, they began dripping down the sides of the buildings, each one energizing itself with a single Twin Turbo-9000 SP5 Kung-Fu Titanium/Lithium Alloy Processor.

As the huge booger chunks oozed closer
and closer, they began sprouting strange-
looking metallic eyeballs and huge,
menacing robotic limbs.

Suddenly, the three Ridiculous Robo-
Boogers leaped toward George, Harold,
Sulu, Mr. Krupp, and Melvin . . .

. . . and the chase was on.

"Oh, NO!" screamed George.

"Here we go again!" screamed Harold.

SNOT AGAIN!!!

Find out if George, Harold, and the gang outrun the Robo-Boogers in Part 2 of this adventure:

COMING SEPTEMBER 30, 2003

Play the Bionic Booger Boy video games at www.pilkey.com.